JOHN B KEANE is one of Ireland's most humorous authors and is recognised as a major Irish playwright. He has written many bestsellers including *Letters of a Successful TD*, *Letters of an Irish Parish Priest*, *Letters of an Irish Publican*, *Letters of a Matchmaker*, *Letters of a Love-Hungry Farmer*, *The Gentle Art of Matchmaking*, *Irish Short Stories*, *More Irish Short Stories*, *The Bodhrán Makers* and *Man of the Triple Name*. His plays include *The Field*, *The Year of the Hiker*, *Big Maggie*, *Sive*, *Sharon's Grave*, *Many Young Men of Twenty*, *The Man from Clare*, *The Change in Mame Fadden*, *Values*, *The Crazy Wall* and *The Buds of Ballybunion*.

"MOLL"

John B. Keane

New Revised Text
edited by
Ben Barnes

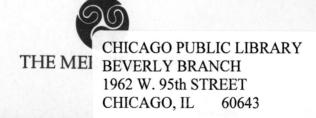

THE MER

THE MERCIER PRESS Ltd, 4 Bridge Street, Cork
24 Lower Abbey Street, Dublin 1

© John B. Keane, 1991

ISBN 0-85342-993-6

A CIP catalogue record for this book
is available from the British Library

Moll is a copyright play and may not be performed without a licence. Application for a licence for amateur performances must be made in advance to The Mercier Press, 4 Bridge Street, Cork. Professional terms may be had from Mr John B. Keane, 37 William Street, Listowel, Co. Kerry.

Printed in Ireland by Colour Books Ltd

This revised version of *Moll* was first presented by Groundwork in association with Gaiety Entertainments at the Gaiety Theatre on 10 June 1991.

Father Brest	Barry McGovern
Bridgie Andover	Joan Brosnan Walsh
Canon Pratt	Mick Lally
Father Loran	Ronan Smith
Moll	Pat Leavy
Ulick	Micheál Ó Briain
The Bishop	Derry Power

Director	Brian de Salvo
Designer	Bláithín Sheerin
Lighting	Rupert Murray

Producers	Ben Barnes
	Arthur Lappin

Executive Producer	Ronan Smith

Moll had its premiere by Theatre of the South, at Killarney on 1 July 1971, and continued at the Opera House, Cork from 26 July 1971.

Father Brest, C.C.	Flor Dullea
Mrs Andover	Kay Healy
Very Rev. Canon Pratt, P.P.	Chris Sheehan
Father Loran, C.C.	Paddy Comerford
Moll	Mary O'Donovan
Bridgie	Mary Foley
Ulick	Denis Harrington
His Lordship the Bishop	James N. Healy

Decor   Patrick Murray

Producer   James N. Healy

ACT ONE

Scene 1

To set a scene or provide an amusing philosophical commentary on the preceding one, a series of extracts from the Canon's diary have been selected with appropriate accompanying action on the forestage. These 'front cloth' vignettes also enable the stage to be set for the following scene and ensure a continual flow of action.

Canon Pratt   After the new money came things were never the same at the presbytery. Till then summers came and summers went each one much like the last. Ballast was a poor parish but God was good and even the weather was good sometimes and we went about our duties without a bother on us.

Until the summer of that fateful year of our Lord nineteen hundred and seventy one when the money went decimal. Oh it had a most shocking and deleterious effect on some people. Why else would our housekeeper of twenty years, the honest, sober, industrious and respectable Letitia Bottomley suddenly up and marry an American tourist and emigrate to New Jersey in the United States of America, there to open a diner which she entitled 'The Black Bottom Bistro'?

Yirra, 'twas the decimal money that drove the poor woman demented and left us with the onerous duty of finding a new housekeeper ....

MOLL

The curtain rises to reveal the dining cum sitting-room of the parochial house in the town and parish of Ballast. Seated at one end of a large table to left of audience but facing them for the most part are three priests. Two are young whereas the one in the middle is elderly and exhibits the purple of a Canon here and there. Seated at the other end of the table at right of audience but fully facing them is a large, dour woman of advanced years. She is Miss Andover. She wears hat and coat and has a large handbag held tightly in front of her. The curates are Father Loran, the younger and Father Brest, the older. The parish priest is Canon Pratt. In front of the priests are neat files to which they resort from time to time. As the curtain rises the priests and Canon are seen to be exchanging whispers and confidences. Miss Andover strains forward trying to catch what they are saying. Father Brest becomes aware of this and alerts others who immediately pay full attention to Miss Andover.

Time: One morning not too long ago.

Father Brest	It says here, Miss Andover, in this most recent reference from the late Father Hennessy that you take a drink on occasion. Does this mean intoxicating drink?
Miss Andover	*(Looks away when she answers)* For all I take of it Father, I don't know why he mentioned it at all, the Lord be good to the man.
Father Brest	Yes, yes …. You do take intoxicating drink however?
Miss Andover	On very rare occasions Father, barring I had a cold or pains or the like.
Father Brest	I see. *(To others)* Any further questions?

8

Canon Pratt	Supposing you were to get the job Miss Andover, would you require extra help?
Miss Andover	Well, I would have to have a maid naturally. There's three of you ….
Canon Pratt	And what sort of salary would you be expecting?
Miss Andover	God knows Canon seeing the way everything's gone up since the money went decimal if I get's the job, I'd need ten pounds a week.
Father Brest	It says here, Miss Andover, that you are a good, natural cook.
Miss Andover	I'm all that Father.
Father Brest	I'm sure you are. Tell me. What is meant by *natural*?
Miss Andover	Yirra, the Lord be good to the poor man Father, he always ate what I put in front of him and there was never a word out of him.
Father Brest	I'm sure he did. It's just that the expression is so unusual. *(To others)* These are not the kind of words that automatically link each other. Usually we hear of plain cooks and excellent cooks. I've even heard of simple cooks but a natural cook … now that's a new one.
Father Loran	*(Entering into the spirit of things)* I see what you mean. Could it be that cooking comes natural to her, that she is a sort of

9

genius at it? *(Uses hand to explain)* Jack Dempsey was a natural fighter and ... take Caruso ... he was a natural singer, sure Jack Doyle was both. Say a fellow goes out and plays golf for the first time and doesn't miss the ball the first swing ... well he's natural.

(There is a sobering cough from Canon Pratt, curates are attentive at once)

Father Loran   Sorry Canon.

Father Brest   *(To Miss Andover)* Now Miss Andover I would like to submit you to a small test.

(Miss Andover jumps up, almost falls, recovers and sits)

Miss Andover   You won't put a hand on me. I was never touched by the hand of a man ....

Father Brest   It's not a physical test. I'll merely mention a particular word or group of words and you say whatever comes into your mind. Do you understand?

Miss Andover   Alright. I'll chance it.

Father Brest   Wardrobe!

Miss Andover   Bottle of Gin!

Father Brest   Sweet tooth!

Miss Andover   Porter Cake!

Father Brest   Sunday morning!

Miss Andover   Gin and Tonic!

Father Brest   Cold in the nose!

Miss Andover	Bloody Mary!
Canon Pratt	Sacristy!
Miss Andover	Altar wine!

(All three exchange knowing looks)

Father Brest   Thank you Miss Andover. We know all we need to know. You'll be hearing from us.

(Exit Miss Andover. Canon Pratt produces a pipe which he proceeds to light. Father Brest rises and lights a cigarette. Father Loran reads through a file)

Father Brest   There's a right wan!

Canon Pratt   The standard's dropped. Good housekeepers are not to be had.

Father Brest   You must remember there's plenty of work in factories and hotels.

Canon Pratt   They don't seem anxious to make a career out of it any more. When I was a young man it was a great temptation to widows and spoiled nuns and the likes … but now they prefer the outside.

Father Brest   But they can have the outside morning, noon and night. A parish priest's housekeeper isn't the same as a nun.

Canon Pratt   *(Thoughtfully)* They used to be. They used to be very like them in manner and in obedience. *(To Brest)* By the way you were on the ball about the drinking.

11

Father Brest	I knew her late employer, Father Dick Hennessy. Dineaway Dick the teachers of the parish used to call him.
Canon Pratt	Why Dineaway?
Father Brest	Don't you see? He never dined at home.
Canon Pratt	Why didn't he say as much in the reference?
Father Brest	He couldn't.
Canon Pratt	Why couldn't he?
Father Brest	Because he wasn't able. The Lord have mercy on the poor man he could never bring himself to say a hard word about anyone.
Canon Pratt	That's why you questioned her about the drink?
Father Brest	Of course. You may be sure if Dick Hennessy said she took a drink on occasion what he really meant was that she was a cross between a wine-taster and a dipsomaniac.
Canon Pratt	And this business about her being a natural cook?
Father Brest	That she served up the food natural, that is to say she didn't bother much with the cooking of it beforehand.
Canon Pratt	Ah....
Father Brest	Gentlemen, we're in a spot. Here we were without a trouble in the world, as

united as three leaves on a shamrock, and as well disposed to each other as if we were brothers and now we are left to look out for ourselves. You'll never know the true worth of a real housekeeper till she's gone. Losing Miss Bottomley was like losing a mother.

Canon Pratt   (*Reverentially*) Lads, do you remember her pickled tongue? Her beef stew?

Father Loran   Her shepherd's pie Canon!

Father Brest   Her stuffed pork!

Father Loran   Her colcannon Canon!

Canon Pratt   Jasus what she couldn't do with a duck! And lads do you remember her cockle and mussel soup? The smell of it, the taste of it.

(They fall silent, basking in the memory of such culinary delights)

Canon Pratt   This is torture lads, sheer torture. Where were we?

Father Loran   (*Holding up a file*) This is the last one.

Canon Pratt   Who is she? Refresh me Joe, will you, like a good man.

Father Loran   Miss Mollie Kettle age forty-seven.

Father Brest   Forty seven, my arse.

Canon Pratt   Well we'll soon find out when we see her. *(To Loran)* Go on Father.

13

Father Loran

Aged forty-seven. Worked as house-keeper in a boys' school in Liverpool, in an old folks' home in Dublin. Worked for nine years as a housekeeper to Monsignor Patrick MacMerrigan. Now retired. She's been idle for three months.

Canon Pratt

Read MacMerrigan's reference. Biggest windbag in the diocese.

Father Loran

(*Locates and reads*) 'Miss Maureen (Mollie) Kettle', the Mollie is in brackets, 'came to work for me on the death of my housekeeper Mrs Sarah O'Hara nine years ago on the precise morning of the two thousandth and twentieth anni-versary of the battle of Pharsalia. Quanti est sapere. She struck me at once as being a woman of integrity. She answer-ed all of my questions satisfactorily and having assured myself that her refer-ences were in order and that she had a reasonable knowledge of the True Faith I employed her forthwith. I found her to be a thrifty and exact housekeeper, a good time-keeper and a faithful servant. I found her to be a good cook and a better punch-maker. I know no more of the good woman nor do I need to, Omne ignotum pro magnifico'. (*Father Loran puts letter aside*) That's the lot.

Father Brest

You were right Canon. He is a windbag.

Canon Pratt

To use a golfing metaphor you will understand Phil, if she could endure Monsignor MacMerrigan for nine holes, she will go the full eighteen with me.

Father Brest This must be approached coldly. *(Moves to centre of table)* If we lose detachment all we gain is a poor housekeeper.

Canon Pratt Of course. Of course. Call her in Joe, like a good man, will you?

(Father Loran rises and goes to door from where he calls)

Father Loran Miss Kettle, will you please come in?

(He returns to his former position as do others. Enter Moll Kettle. Middle-aged. Wears hat and coat, carries handbag)

Father Brest *(Indicates chair vacated by Miss Andover)* Please be seated.

(Moll takes a seat and waits, smiling serenely in all directions)

Father Brest *(Coughs)* Well now. It's a nice day out Miss Kettle, isn't it?

Moll It is, thanks be to God, a very nice day entirely Canon.

Canon Pratt Allow me to introduce my two curates, Father Brest and Father Loran. It's possible they may want to ask a question or two but be at your ease, be at your ease. This isn't an inquisition. I see here that you seem to have met with Monsignor MacMerrigan's approval.

Moll We got on great.

Father Brest	And the new Monsignor?
Moll	I couldn't tell you nothing about him Father.
Father Brest	Isn't it a wonder now you didn't stay on with him?
Moll	He didn't ask me Father.
Father Brest	And why not?
Moll	He brought his own woman with him Father.
Father Brest	You haven't worked for three months. Isn't that a long time to be without a job?
Moll	'Tis indeed Father, a long time surely.
Father Brest	Is it how you couldn't get a job?
Moll	I could get a job alright.
Father Brest	And why didn't you take one?
Moll	After working nine years with a Monsignor 'tisn't every job I *would* take. I couldn't bring myself to work with no less than a Canon. 'Twould be a great come-down to me after all my years to have to fall into work with an ordinary priest.
Father Brest	(*Looks to others for approval, laughs*) That's a very odd reason!
Canon Pratt	I don't know. I don't see anything odd about it.

16

Moll	'Tis hard Canon, to come back to the plain black and white when one is used to the purple. Meaning no offence ….
Canon Pratt	No indeed. No indeed. And tell me now Miss Kettle, would you need help? What I mean is would you need an assistant?
Moll	An assistant Canon?
Canon Pratt	A maidservant to help you.
Moll	I wouldn't leave one of 'em inside the door. A maidservant with curates in the house! We'll leave well enough alone Canon.
Canon Pratt	How right you are Miss Kettle. What sort of a wage would you be expecting?
Moll	Eight pounds a week Canon, and if we didn't fall out you might see your way to giving me a rise after a year or two.
Canon Pratt	I might so. I might so.
Father Brest	Have you any hobbies?
Moll	Bingo Father. Only on the Sunday night, and the television now and then.
Father Brest	The disease of bingo: I see faith. Well we haven't been invaded by that particular malady in this parish yet and if I have my way we never will.
Father Loran	Might I ask a question?
Canon Pratt	I suppose so.

17

Father Loran	What do you think of Vatican Two?
Moll	What's that Father?
Father Loran	Vatican Two. What do you think of it?
Moll	Hawaii–Five–O is my own favourite Father.
Canon Pratt	Now, now Father. You mustn't expect the good woman to know about these things. Tell me Miss Kettle, when could you begin work … that is if we decided to take you on?
Moll	I could come in the morning Canon.
Canon Pratt	I see. Well lads, any more questions?
Father Brest	I presume Monsignor MacMerrigan had curates.
Moll	He had Father, three of 'em.
Father Brest	And did you get references from those?
Moll	I did not indeed.
Father Brest	And why not?
Moll	No one takes notice of a curate's reference Father.
Father Brest	Huh?
Father Loran	Nobody!
Moll	Well nobody except another curate.
	(*The Canon seems to enjoy this*)
Father Brest	No more questions.

MOLL

Canon Pratt	Very well then. Miss Kettle would you be good enough to wait outside for a few minutes? I assure you we won't keep you long.
	(Moll takes handbag, folds arms and exits. The Canon rises and stands with his back to fireplace)
Canon Pratt	Now's the time to say it lads.
Father Brest	I don't know ....
Canon Pratt	What don't you know?
Father Brest	There's something about her.
Father Loran	I think she's alright. She's not very bright but she's alright.
Father Brest	*(Rises and paces)* Now that's where I disagree entirely with you. You say she's not very bright I say otherwise. She may give the impression that she's not bright but I say she's a lot sharper than she lets on to be.
Canon Pratt	And what if she is? So long as she fits the bill what else matters? I may tell you Phil, that I think we would be damned lucky to have her.
Father Loran	I agree
Canon Pratt	Come on Phil, make it unanimous.
Father Brest	I wish I could. This woman frightens me. There's something hidden beneath that calm surface. She's too quick with her answers.

19

Father Loran	Now Phil ….
Father Brest	No Joe. I'm seriously concerned. When a presbytery gets a new housekeeper it's like a regiment that gets a new sergeant major. A new housekeeper is like a new moon and a new moon can bring anything from a tidal wave to an earthquake.
Canon Pratt	You're an alarmist Phil.
Father Brest	Maybe but I have a foreboding. In these matters I'm as sensitive as a seismograph.
Father Loran	A what?
Father Brest	Seismograph!
Father Loran	Oh, yes.
Father Brest	And already I am recording the first faint vibrations of a calamity that is about to befall. I am registering the first awful rumblings of a collapsing presbytery.

(Others laugh, Father Brest sits)

Canon Pratt	Spare the flowery language for Sunday's sermon Father.
Father Brest	Alright but don't forget I warned you.
Canon Pratt	Are we agreed then?
Others	Agreed.
Canon Pratt	I'm glad that we're decided. I think we

chose wisely. (*Canon moves to the door*) Miss Kettle, will you come in please?

(*Moll enters*)

Canon Pratt Will you be good enough to take a seat Miss Kettle?

(*Moll sits*)

Canon Pratt Your Christian name is Maureen, is it not?

Moll That's right Canon although them that knows me calls me 'Moll'.

Canon Pratt 'Moll' is it? Well now Moll, we have good news for you girl. Whenever you're ready you can begin work. The salary is agreed. I'm sorry it's not more but we are a very poor parish with a new school to be built and repairs to the church and God knows what else.

Moll 'Tis alright Canon. I'm sure I'll manage — as I've always done.

Canon Pratt I dare say we might agree that a month's notice either way would be reasonable, in case things don't work out.

Moll Ah, they'll work out fine Canon, you'll see.

Canon Pratt Very well then. If you'll come with me I'll show you the layout of the place

(*Canon rises and indicates other exit. Moll rises*)

21

Moll	*(To all)* I hope now please God that it will be the lucky day for all of us.
Canon Pratt	Yes, please God.
Father Loran	Please God.
Canon Pratt	Of course we have a handy man and then there's the parish clerk and as you say ….

(Exit Moll and Canon)

Father Loran	For better or for worse we have ourselves a housekeeper. *(Collects papers)*
Father Brest	I've said my piece. Only time can tell. I hope for your sake and mine I'm proved wrong.
Father Loran	I think you're being ridiculous, now, you know. *(Crosses to fireplace, puts papers away on top of pouffe there)*
Father Brest	Remember that I am a veteran of five presbyteries and I happen to know that God's greatest blessing is a good housekeeper but that God's greatest curse is a bad one. I haven't met a bad one yet but I know men who have. They died from malnutrition. This woman strikes me as a bad one. I could be wrong but I feel it in my bones and my bones have yet to let me down. I have to go. I'll see you later. *(Moves to door down left)*
Father Loran	Where are you going?

Father Brest   I'm going for a round of golf if you must know but first I'm going out to the chapel and in the chapel I propose to go down on my two knees and commence a novena for the salvation of all of us, not to any saint and not to any martyr but straight through, no messing and no diversions, straight through to God the Father Almighty Himself. Be seein' you.

(Exits)

Bridge ACT ONE Scene 1 to Scene 2

Canon Pratt   Of the many afflictions that annoy the human condition the poisonous canker of Doubt seems to me one of the most potent and least recognised. And Doubt has an insidious and deadly effect upon the infected person bringing torment to the soul and encouraging a terrible railing against the will of God, erupting in fits of rage.

For my part I thank God for the blessing of Optimism. And my faith in Optimism was never better justified than in the case of Moll Kettle. For when I offered the opinion that we had chosen wisely in appointing her as our housekeeper my words were clearly divinely inspired ...

Action takes place as before. The time is morning, a month later. The priests and Canon are seated at table breakfasting. The Canon is eating heartily, Father Loran not so heartily and Father Brest not at all. Moll enters with bowl of black and white pudding.

Moll   Excuse me Canon. *(Loads Canon's plate)*

Canon Pratt   Watch out, I'll burst.

Moll   Just a little more. Is the breakfast alright Canon?

Canon Pratt   Fine, fine, couldn't be better. How long are you with us now Moll?

Moll   A month yesterday Canon.

24

Canon Pratt	*(Heartily)* A month yesterday, faith. Well, now does time be long in passing? Off with you Moll. We're fine here.
Moll	Thank you Canon. *(Is about to exit)* What about the dinner Canon?
Canon Pratt	We'll leave that entirely to yourself Moll.
Moll	Would bacon and turnips be alright then?
Canon Pratt	Bacon and turnips would be glorious Moll, just glorious.
Moll	Thank you Canon.
	(Exits)
Canon Pratt	There's a great woman.
Father Brest	I don't know all about that.
Canon Pratt	*(Still eating away heartily)* You haven't hit it off with her Phil, have you?
Father Brest	Quite frankly, no.
Canon Pratt	Well we mustn't let it spoil our break-fast.
	(Canon resumes eating. Father Loran nibbles. Father Brest does not eat but with his knife probes through objects on his plate. He frowns. He bends over plate, exaggeratedly peering at contents, finally he lifts up a tiny object. He holds it in front of him)
Father Brest	Father Loran?
Father Loran	Yes Father Brest.

25

Father Brest   You're a man who has excellent eye-sight.

Father Loran   Well, I don't need spectacles anyway, thanks be to God.

Father Brest   That's good. Perhaps you could tell me what this is which I am holding in my hand. Take your time now ....

(Father Loran looks carefully at object and shakes his head)

Father Loran   It beats me.

Father Brest   Does it remind you of anything?

Father Loran   Offhand I can't say.

Father Brest   Here take it in your hand and make a careful examination.

(Father Loran accepts object and turns it over in his hand)

Father Brest   Interesting, isn't it?

Father Loran   It certainly is. I must confess I'm baffled. *(Holds it out in front of him)* I honestly can't say what it is.

Father Brest   Have you ever seen anything like it before?

Father Loran   *(More examination)* N ... No. I can't say that I have.

Father Brest   Hand it back, please. It could be valu-able.

Father Loran   Valuable?

Father Brest	Museums and universities are always interested in curiosities.
Canon Pratt	*(Crossly)* Do I detect a note of sarcasm Father Brest, because if I do I may tell you here and now I won't have it. What in blazes are you on about then?
Father Brest	*(Exhibits rasher)* It's this.
Canon Pratt	*(Suspiciously)* What is it?
Father Brest	I wish I knew.
	(The Canon peers closely at it)
Canon Pratt	Damn and blast it man, that's a rasher.
Father Brest	Is it?
Canon Pratt	It is of course.
Father Brest	But it's too small to be a rasher.
Canon Pratt	It's still a rasher.
Father Brest	*(Irked)* It must have come off a bloody banbh.
Father Loran	Or a pyg ... my.
Canon Pratt	What?
Father Loran	Get it, a pygmy, hah?
Canon Pratt	*(Conciliatory)* Come on Phil. Stop the nonsense and eat your breakfast, like a good boy.
Father Brest	What breakfast?

27

Canon Pratt	The breakfast on your plate. I see nothing wrong with it.
Father Brest	What you mean is there's nothing wrong with yours. You did alright for yourself. Look at the size of your sausages and look at the size of ours. *(He holds up a sausage)* What do you think of that?
Father Loran	Normal sausages run about sixteen to the pound. Forty-eight of these wouldn't make a pound. Of course I don't mind. I haven't much of an appetite anyway but it's tough on poor Phil Canon.
Father Brest	You're bloody sure it's tough on poor Phil.
Canon Pratt	Maybe they are what are known as cocktail sausages. It's a fact you know that there could be more nourishment in a small meaty, hardy sort of a sausage than you'd get out of a big, fat, soft one.
Father Brest	*(Sarcastically)* Is that a fact?
Canon Pratt	Oh, yes indeed. Isn't there a saying to cover it, what in blazes is it again ... something to do with parcels.
Father Loran	The best of goods come in small parcels.
Canon Pratt	That's the one. Good man Joe. There's a lot to some of these old sayings, you know.
Father Brest	Fair enough then I'll tell you what we'll do. In future you can have the small

hardy sausages and I'll take the big, fat ones.

Canon Pratt   What's gotten into you lately Phil?

Father Brest   It's the housekeeper, your precious Moll. She seems to think the curates can live on the wind.

Canon Pratt   Now, now the poor woman does the best she can.

Father Brest   She does the best she can for you.

Canon Pratt   That's your imagination.

Father Brest   Is it ...? (*Sticks a fork in the Canon's remaining sausage. Sticks fork in one of his own sausages*) Have a look Canon. Now is it my imagination? Am I seeing things Canon, or is one of those sausages three times as large as the other? Am I seeing things Father Loran?

Father Loran   You are *not*.

Father Brest   Am I Canon ...?

Canon Pratt   If you want fat sausages why in blazes don't you ask for fat sausages?

Father Brest   (*Returning sausages*) Alright, I'm asking for them now.

Canon Pratt   (*Coldly*) Very good. You've made your point. May we proceed with our breakfasts?

Father Brest   You proceed by all means but I have something more to say.

Canon Pratt

(Eating calmly) You'd better get it off your chest then, hadn't you?

Father Brest

Yes. I had better hadn't I?

(Father Brest rises. Father Loran would caution him to use restraint but Brest has the floor)

Father Brest

That woman in there, that so-called housekeeper has deliberately gone out of her way to make my life a misery since she came here a month ago. I was an easy-going placid man, a happy man in a happy house, content with my fare and with my lot and then she comes slowly, insidiously, poisonously she tries to break me....

Canon Pratt

What a vivid imagination you have Phil.

Father Brest

Have I? Have you heard her when she calls me? I'm relaxed and happy and then suddenly in the distance I hear the shriek ... *(Imitates shrill, shrieking voice)* 'Father Brest, Father Bre-est', I tell you I'm shattered.

Canon Pratt

For God's sake Phil, gather hold of yourself. The poor woman has nothing against you.

Father Brest

Hasn't she? Did I hear you agree to bacon and turnips for lunch today ...?

Canon Pratt

Yes ... but we can always change it if you want to ....

Father Brest

I know what I'll get today. I'll get the

	stringiest, toughest, smallest piece of the whole lot. Something leathery and lardy from the middle of an old sow's belly.
Father Loran	So will I.
Father Brest	*(To Loran angrily)* Yes, but you have no appetite and I have. *(To Canon)* You watch it now at lunchtime … just see for yourself if I'm exaggerating … in the interests of common justice have a look at my plate.
Canon Pratt	Why don't you have a talk with her?
Father Brest	I would never demean myself by talking with a creature like that.
Canon Pratt	Oh, dear me, we're very perturbed this morning.
Father Brest	*(Spreading hands out for calm and reasoning)* Alright. You remember yesterday's lunch?
Canon Pratt	*(Reluctantly)* Yes.
Father Brest	What did it consist of?
Canon Pratt	I have an atrocious memory.
Father Brest	I'll help you. Were there some lamb chops?
Canon Pratt	I believe there were some lamb chops.
Father Brest	The exact number Canon?
Canon Pratt	I think there were three.

Father Brest	So there were three. Good. May I ask what else was on the plate?
Canon Pratt	*(Thoughtfully)* Peas I believe. Yes, I'm certain there were some peas.
Father Brest	How many peas?
Canon Pratt	*(Laughs)* Oh, now Phil, I didn't count them ....
Father Brest	Of course you didn't. As I recall you had a very large plate. In fact I would not be wrong if I said that it was more of a dish than a plate ....
Canon Pratt	*(Irritation)* Go on. Go on.
Father Brest	Half the dish was taken up by the three lamb cutlets. What my dear Canon, took up the rest of the area of the plate?
Canon Pratt	*(Sighs)* Peas I said but what's the point Father?
Father Brest	So we may presume that an area of almost one square foot was entirely covered by peas. How many peas would you say there were in this area of the plate?
Canon Pratt	*(Severely)* Alright, there were a few hundred peas or thereabouts. I can't be certain.
Father Brest	Thank you Canon. You have been most helpful. Now did you see what was on my plate Canon?
Canon Pratt	No. I did not. I had something better to do.

Father Brest	Oh begob, you had! What was on my plate Father Loran? And please speak up.

(Loran tries to speak but Brest flows on)

Father Brest	I want you to be heard. Now what was on my plate Father?
Father Loran	*(Entering into the spirit of the thing)* There was what appeared to be one small mutton chop or some article which outwardly resembled a small mutton chop. It was, if I may say so, the smallest mutton chop I have ever seen ....
Father Brest	Go on please. What else Father?
Father Loran	There also appeared to be a small quantity of what seemed to me to be tinned peas.
Father Brest	Could we be a little bit more specific Father? Take your time but be honest in your answer.
Father Loran	It is my honest opinion that there were twenty peas on the plate.
Father Brest	You are wrong Father. I counted those peas and instead of twenty there were nineteen peas. Is this fair Canon? Is this honest Canon?
Canon Pratt	I'll talk to her. I had no hand in it I assure you. I'll talk to her this very day.
Father Brest	I believe you but before I close let me add that I could not chew the meat of

33

that chop yesterday. I tried and failed. I hacked at it and I tore at it but I made no impression. I can only conclude that the same chop which I euphemistically call-ed mutton was not mutton at all. *(Goes furiously towards exit where he stands)* I can only conclude that it was hacked, gartered and hewn from the posterior of a mountain ram who was siring ewes when Holy Saint Patrick was a boy in the mountains of Antrim.

(Exits)

Canon Pratt	By the Lord but that was a mighty outburst Joe.
Father Loran	He's been complaining with a bit.
Canon Pratt	That's the first I heard.
Father Loran	I suppose he kept it in for too long, hence the unexpected explosion.
Canon Pratt	And do you agree with him?
Father Loran	Well, I do and I don't.
Canon Pratt	Well, do you or don't you?
Father Loran	Well, I think I do but on the other hand ....
Canon Pratt	I'll have a talk with her.

(In the distance can be heard the high pitched sound of Moll's voice calling Father Brest)

Father Loran	No time like the present. Here she comes. I'll skedaddle.

(Enter Moll)

Moll	Where's Father Brest?
Canon Pratt	Who wants him?
Moll	There's a sick call.
Father Loran	I'll take it Miss Kettle.
Moll	Very well. The man is waiting outside.
Father Loran	The ball is at your feet Canon. Watch how you kick.

(Exits)

Canon Pratt	Moll will you sit down for a minute? I want to have a little talk with you.
Moll	Very good Canon. *(Moll takes a seat)*
Canon Pratt	Moll ... poor Father Brest is very perturbed.
Moll	Oh the poor man, I hope he'll get out of it!
Canon Pratt	He thinks you're cutting down on his food. So does Father Loran but Loran doesn't seem to mind.
Moll	Enough is enough Canon and I've always given the pair of them enough. Maybe 'tis how they expect the same as yourself.
Canon Pratt	That's just it Moll. They do and they have every right to expect it.
Moll	Have they no respect for seniority?

Canon Pratt All I know is that Father Brest maintains he is not getting enough to eat. Now what have you to say to that?

Moll Your last housekeeper Canon, spent forty pounds a month on meat alone for this household. That much money would keep a company of soldiers in meat. Forty pounds on meat alone.

Canon Pratt Was it that much?

Moll Every penny of it Canon.

Canon Pratt And how much was it this month Moll?

Moll Ten pounds Canon.

Canon Pratt Great God Moll but you're a pure magician. And the food was never better. *(Corrects himself)* My food was never better. And did you cut down much on the other items Moll?

Moll I did indeed Canon. The grocery bill is cut by half.

Canon Pratt Great God but you're a genius entirely Moll. Still we have this problem about Father Brest.

Moll God save us all Canon but 'tis wrong to give young priests too much to eat.

Canon Pratt Why would you say that Moll?

Moll Because they get notions Canon.

Canon Pratt Notions Moll?

36

Moll   Notions Canon. Over in Scotland Canon
            a few years ago a young curate rose up
            one morning without his collar and went
            off with a half-naked lady acrobat.

Canon Pratt   Ah, go on ....

Moll   A lady acrobat. 'Twas in the papers
            Canon. Beef Canon, and steaks that was
            half raw was the cause of it. That was
            what Monsignor MacMerrigan's doctor
            told us. He knew the curate. If 'twas
            plain bread and butter and gravy he was
            getting he'd be too weak to get notions.

Canon Pratt   I dare say there's something in what you
            say Moll.

Moll   In the name of God Canon, will you look
            at the jaunty cut of them two hardy
            bucks.

Canon Pratt   Ah, now they're young and they're ....

Moll   Isn't that what I'm at Canon?

Canon Pratt   Huh?

Moll   Two prime bucks and they have the gall
            to look for more food. Sure if they eat
            any more they'll go out of their minds
            altogether. If you feed them like game-
            cocks they'll crow like gamecocks and
            they'll strut like gamecocks.

Canon Pratt   And you think they're getting enough?

Moll   Are they priests or are they gluttons
            Canon? Is there nothing else to life but

their gullets? Would you hear the Pope asking for lamb cutlets? When Cardinal Monsooki from Persia came to see the Monsignor two years ago, did he ask for lamb cutlets? He did not indeed. A plate of giblet soup and a crust of bread was all the poor man had and he a Cardinal. Yet we have two pampered bucks of curates looking for lamb cutlets, begrudging their own Canon the bit he does be eating. What worries have them two beyond the filling of their bellies? Have they to think about the education of children and the building of schools or is their guts their only concern?

Canon Pratt   I can't answer you Moll. In all truth Moll, I can't answer you.

Moll   (*She rises and starts to tidy table*) And will you tell me another thing Canon?

Canon Pratt   I will if I can Moll.

Moll   The church Canon. There's three holes in the roof, Canon, and the windows are rotten. Are the people of the parish Canon, to be exposed to rain and cold and draughts because Father Brest don't like bingo?

Canon Pratt   The people of the parish must come before all else Moll, before me, you, before anybody.

Moll   Would you like to see the old people catching pneumonia when they kneel down to say their prayers? Is that what

38

you want Canon? Is it how you want the feeble and the delicate to be bent over with pain, and them that has weak joints to be crippled?

Canon Pratt 'Tis not what I want Moll.

Moll We'll be all racked with pleurisy and T.B. if them holes in the roof aren't seen to. And why Canon? Will you tell me why?

Canon Pratt Because Father Brest doesn't like bingo.

Moll And does he like bridge Canon?

Canon Pratt By all accounts he's a dab hand at it Moll.

Moll And golf Canon. Don't he play golf?

Canon Pratt He plays golf. In fact he has won tournaments Moll.

Moll So 'tis alright for Father Brest and his equals to play golf and bridge.

Canon Pratt Yes. 'Tis alright for them.

Moll (*About to exit with hands full of breakfast things*) But 'tis not alright for the poor people of this parish to play an innocent game of bingo.

(*Enter Brest in a hurry*)

Father Brest Well did you have a talk with Moll about the food?

Canon Pratt	Indeed I did — we're putting a new roof on the church.
Father Brest	What's that got to do with it — where are you going to get the money?
Canon Pratt	*You're* going to get it Father Brest. From now on you're in charge of the bingo.

(Moll laughs and exits)

Bridge ACT ONE Scene 2 to Scene 3

Canon Pratt   If there is a sound that pleases me more than most 'tis the sound of laughter. Laughter erupts from the soul in an irrepressible declamation of an excess of good humour.

Laughter is natural, you see. 'Tis one of the many magical gifts the good Lord provides. The warmth of the sun, the whisper of the trees, the murmur of the sea. The nectar of the very air we breathe. Go right ahead, says the Lord. 'Tis free. Enjoy it.

The time is evening of a day several months after the arrival of Moll Kettle. Moll is dusting. As she dusts the several chairs they bring to her mind her impressions of the three who normally sit in them. Then she goes to dust a picture behind the door down left and while she is there the two curates burst in, concealing her behind it.

Father Brest   We made it *(Shakes Loran's hand)* Congratulations *(Loran puzzled)* on evading you know who. I'll ring the mother while I have the chance. She's taken to listening in on telephone calls now *(Picks up the phone to dial)* The other night I was on to her and in the middle of the conversation I sensed there was someone in the vicinity. *(Puts down phone)*

Father Loran   And was she there?

Father Brest She was standing behind the door of this very room.

(With his back to it slams the door. Loran sees Moll, but Brest doesn't)

Father Brest Still as a statue, hardly breathing, with an innocent look on her face as if she weren't listening at all.

(Loran gestures, Brest turns and sees Moll)

Father Brest What are you doing there?

Moll Doing where boybawn?

Father Brest Doing there; hiding behind the door.

Moll Cobwebs, I'm hunting cobwebs. The presbytery is draped with them.

Father Brest Do you realise that I was making a phone call to my mother? You were eavesdropping again, you ought to be ashamed of yourself.

Would you mind leaving the room now so that I can ring my mother?

Moll I'll go boybawn when I have the cobwebs cleared.

Father Brest You'll go now!

Moll I was here before you.

Father Brest If you don't leave this room instantly I will remove you forcibly.

Father Loran Keep your temper! No violence.

Moll	I'm going to say a rosary for the poor souls — but remember one thing ….
Father Brest	What would that be?
Moll	A call to your mother is not church business.
Father Brest	Meaning what?
Moll	Meaning that you can leave the money for the call beside the phone.
	(She exits in triumph)
Father Loran	Well, mother love is a wonderful thing — but it will cost you money from now on.
Father Brest	May God forgive me but I can't bear that woman. *(On phone)* Get me Castletownbere 49.
Father Loran	*(Putting his coat and hat on small table upstage)* We are supposed to show meekness and sufferance in the face of adversity. Our first function is forbearance.
Father Brest	It's me or she and by the Lord Heavens it's not going to be me … no, no miss, not you … I mean it's going to be me or she … all right, ring me back *(Puts down phone)*
Father Loran	Well, what was it you were going to tell me?
Father Brest	*(Tossing down a letter)* What do you think of that?

43

Father Loran   What is it?

Father Brest   Take a look.

Father Loran   *(Reluctantly takes out the letter)* You wrote to Monsignor MacMerrigan!

Father Brest   I did.

Father Loran   *(Reading)* He's in rare form alright … 'let me say that you have an irrational impertinence which will land you in hot water some day. So you want further information about Moll Kettle. If you must know she was a great woman entirely. She ran the presbytery on a pittance and if there were more like her there wouldn't be half the trouble in the Church today. You are an impatient and ungodly fellow to want to belittle this woman. Prayer is the last hope for you, prayer and meditation. I need not add fasting because Moll Kettle will see to that. Ha. Ha. May God succour you Father and your many Godless equals. The Church is at the crossroads. Make sure you follow the right path. Yours in J.C. Monsignor Patrick MacMerrigan.' *(Returns the letter)*

Father Brest   How did an old bags like that come to be a Monsignor?

Father Loran   Probably fit for nothing else.

Father Brest   I also wrote to two of his curates.

Father Loran   I thought there were three.

Father Brest	There were but one died shortly after Moll left.
Father Loran	From what?
Father Brest	From a mixture of maleficence, malnutrition and pernicious anaemia.
Father Loran	That last one. What is it?
Father Brest	It's what you and I will die from if we don't get to her first.
Father Loran	That's nice. Did you get replies to those letters?
Father Brest	I did.
Father Loran	Show us.

(Brest is about to hand over both, but on second thoughts retains one and reads it out himself)

Father Brest   This is from Father Paddy O'Shaughnessy who was the senior curate in Moll's early time with MacMerrigan. *(Reads)* 'Dear Phil, Good to hear from you. Saw where you won the West Cork fourball. Congrats. I heard a great night was had by all and you had to be carried .... *(Brest stops and edits the next section of the letter)* About our friend to whom I will not refer by name as I would put nothing past her, not even the steaming open of this letter...'

Father Loran   I don't doubt him. I don't doubt him one bit.

Father Brest   Quiet ... (*Reads*) 'I am, as you know from our student days, a more than passable linguist. In point of fact I now speak four languages fluently. I have a fair knowledge of seven others but in the entire eleven there is no word or group of words which would adequately describe the demon in your midst. Cunning, sharp, deadly, evil itself personified. In the early days of the human species before language was needed she would have been eliminated by what bookmakers refer to as tick-tack. My current choice of foods is grossly restricted from the beating she gave my stomach. You know me Phil. We got on, you and I, but lest there be any doubt in your mind about you know who remember Father Paul Mannick, our dear departed colleague.'

Father Loran   Is that the third one?

Father Brest   Yes.

Father Loran   Requiescat in Pace.

Father Brest   'If he could shed the boards and the brown cloths that bind him and rise from the grave he would point a bony finger in the direction of a certain woman whose name is known to all of us. I conclude. Yours fondly, Father Paddy O'Shaughnessy. P.S. In the honour of God either burn or ate this epistle.'

Father Loran   Cogent.

46

Father Brest	Most cogent.
Father Loran	Tells its own tale.
Father Brest	Forcibly.
Father Loran	Agreed.
Father Brest	*(Proudly)* However that last letter from the middle curate as he styles himself, tells all succinctly and savagely.
Father Loran	*(Reading)* 'Dear Father Brest, I am only the middle curate. You should not involve me. I am neither craven nor cowardly but remember that she who is your housekeeper today could be mine tomorrow. *(Look of alarm at Brest)* For this reason, I am afraid to say more but I'll put it this way. If I were sending a telegram it would say "abandon ship". Sincerely, Robert Connors, C.C.' *(Returns letter)*
Father Brest	Paints a strange picture, does it not?
Father Loran	Weird. What are we going to do?
Father Brest	There's only one thing we can do.
Father Loran	What's that?
Father Brest	The Bishop.
Father Loran	You mean a visit?
Father Brest	Not necessarily, a confidential letter would do.
Father Loran	That's pretty drastic.

Father Brest   She's been with us four months and already I have conducted fifty sessions of bingo, each lasting four hours. I have lost fifteen pounds in weight. I have become a martyr to malnutrition. It will have to be the Bishop. A joint letter.

Father Loran   Count me out.

Father Brest   You can't opt out. We have to make a stand.

Father Loran   It won't work.

Father Brest   Why not?

Father Loran   Because once you've written one letter to the Bishop you can never do it again. Suppose we write to him and tell him the truth about Moll, we will forever after, in his eyes, be the two curates who complained about the food. If sometime either one of us has another complaint to make, he'll say to himself that is one of the two who complained before. You get it?

Father Brest   No. I don't get it. We have a genuine grouse.

Father Loran   But have we? There's plenty bread and butter. There's milk and there are potatoes. No scarcity of essentials if you know what I mean. If the Bishop investigates he's not going to do so without informing the Canon and informing the Canon, as we both know, is the same as

48

informing Moll. She'll be ready for the Bishop. Is it a woman that fobbed off Cardinal Monsooki with watery giblet soup?

Father Brest You won't sign then?

Father Loran Let's wait. If things get worse I'll reconsider. We have very little to show you know; we have no proof. Honestly, Phil, you may have lost weight but you were overeating. You've never looked as fit. Your belly's gone. You're not flabby anymore.

Father Brest I'm living off my fat, I tell you, and when that runs out it's only a matter of time until the major collapse. Hush ... *(To door)* what was that?

(Both men become alert and listen carefully. Brest opens door slightly, Loran comes up behind him. Both listen, Brest turns)

Father Loran It sounds like the banshee to me.

Father Brest Worse. It's the voice of Moll Kettle. Listen ....

(Again they both listen and after a little while unmistakably Moll's voice can be heard)

Moll Father Bre-est ... where are you? ... Father Bre-est.

Father Brest There's no escape. *(Produces letters)* Let's burn this lot.

(He opens and crumbles them, helped by Father Loran. They light the pile)

Father Loran Give them to me and I'll burn them. *(At fireplace)* Here she is.

(Enter Moll)

Moll Father Bre-e .... Oh, there you are!

Father Brest What's the matter now?

Moll The matter is that there's a sick call and there's no priest to take it.

Father Brest We're off-duty.

Moll One of you is supposed to be on call.

Father Brest The Canon is also a priest, you know. He was ordained too, the same as Father Loran and myself.

Moll The Canon went to bed an hour ago with a cold in the head and I have no notion of sending him traipsing into the countryside not knowing would he catch his death of pneumonia.

Father Brest Where is the sick call?

Moll Hurry on. The man is waiting at the door of the presbytery. Hurry on before some poor soul faces his maker without a priest. *(Goes out door)*

Father Brest There's no peace to be had any more.

Moll *(Comes back)* Wouldn't it be nice now if the Bishop heard there was no priest to take a sick call? Suppose I didn't bother searching. 'Tis not my duty you know to locate missing curates. *(Goes out)*

Father Brest   That will do you now. Enough guff, thank you.

Moll   *(Comes back)* What's the bonfire for?

Father Loran   Just some waste Miss Kettle. 'Tis alright.

Father Brest   I don't see that it's any of your business.

Moll   Waste paper that had to be burned. Ha! Ha! That must have been the hot paper.

Father Brest   If it wasn't hot before it's hot now.

Moll   *(About to exit)* You'd better hurry and don't forget the two of you are on the bingo tonight in the parish hall.

Father Brest   Tonight is Wednesday — there's no bingo.

Moll   There's a special session tonight for the Church Holiday.

Father Brest   And I was playing golf with the Doctor.

Father Loran   And I was playing records for the Reverend Mother ....

Moll   Well now, legs eleven, the Doc can go play golf with the Reverend Mother; because tonight the pair of yous are on the bingo. Check!

(Exits)

Bridge ACT ONE Scene 3 to Scene 4

Canon Pratt

A word about the bingo. Bingo is no sin. There are some who will tell you that bingo is gambling and that therefore bingo is a pernicious evil preying upon the vulnerability of simple people.

Yirra, bingo is not gambling at all but a harmless bit o'fun. The prizes are modest and, though welcome, unlikely to launch a winner into the perilous seas of high finance, particularly since there is every encouragement to reinvest in the parish funds for the glorification of God and the salvation of the donor's soul.

Moll at the telephone.

Moll

(On phone) There's none of the curates here now. *(Listens)* Oh! The Canon is resting and can't be disturbed .... *(Listens)* You must talk to him ... a matter of life and death? Listen here to me now. Father Loran is at choir practice. Father Brest is in bed. I'm not going to call the Canon unless there's anointing to be done. What's up with you anyway? *(Listens)* You're pregnant? Well that's hardly the fault of the Canon. *(Listens)* Yes? Yes? You had a right to think of that my dear girl before you let him put the honey in your coffee. *(Listens)* A what? He gave you a green cough drop and told you

52

	'twas the pill. You must be a right eejit. *(Puts down the phone)*
Bridgie	*(Coming in)* 'Tis me. The Canon isn't in, I suppose, is he? I suppose he isn't, is he?
Moll	Weren't you one of the women in for this job?
Bridgie	That's right. No hard feelings.
Moll	What can I do for you?
Bridgie	*(Sits down)* I want to see one of the curates.
Moll	They're not here now.
Bridgie	*(Sits left of table)* The Canon will do just as well.
Moll	The Canon is resting.
Bridgie	Oh dear! That's a pity.
Moll	Maybe I might be able to help. I often stands in for the Canon. Out with it now, whatever it is.
Bridgie	I'm thinking of getting married.
Moll	Are you in earnest?
Bridgie	Oh, I am!
Moll	And who is he?
Bridgie	*(Calls)* Ulick ... Ulick love ... come in and let the woman see you ....

(Enter a man of advanced years, wearing a

cap and long overcoat. He is the very epitome of deference. He wears strong-lensed specs)

Bridgie   He's very shy.

Moll   Will you sit down sir?

(He smiles and shrugs his way out of doing so)

Moll   Are you sure you want to go ahead?

Bridgie   What's wrong with him?

Moll   He'll die on the job.

Bridgie   If he do, won't I have my widow's pension!

Moll   What do you want to get married for anyway?

Bridgie   I have to.

Moll   You have to? Miracles will never cease. There's hope for us all. *(To Ulick)* Shove out here wonder-boy till I have a look at you.

Bridgie   Shove out Ulick, and let the woman have a look at you.

Moll   Are you sure he's the man?

Bridgie   He's the best I could get. I'm no chicken, you know.

Moll   Will you answer an honest question?

54

Bridgie	Of course.
Moll	Are you long gone?
Bridgie	Long gone where?
Moll	You know where.
Bridgie	I don't, honest I don't.
Moll	How many months?
Bridgie	What are you talking about?
Moll	You said you had to get married.
Bridgie	*(Goes into paroxysm of laughter)* Did you hear that Ulick? What she's pinning on you? Yirra get on with ya. I have to get married because I can't get a job. I spent my life working for priests and here I am penniless in the end.
Moll	God knows 'tis true. And did you save anything?
Bridgie	Save on what a priest would pay? You must be mad. The same thing will happen to you some day unless you look out for yourself.
Moll	*(Thoughtfully)* There's a lot to what you say. You've put me thinking, God knows.
Bridgie	How much to get married anyway?
Moll	Two pounds a cow, ten shillings a bullock, five bob a sheep, two bob a goat and a shilling a pig.

Bridgie	How many cows have you Ulick?
	(Ulick lifts four fingers of left hand and holds up other hand clenched)
Bridgie	Four cows and a bull.
Moll	Eight pounds. Yerra give me a fiver and I'll come round the Canon. You gave me good advice. If I don't look out for myself the Canon won't.
Bridgie	Have you a fiver handy Ulick?
	(Ulick locates purse and extracts a fiver, Bridgie takes it and hands it to Moll, who accepts it)
Moll	Let the two of you be here next Monday morning at eight o'clock. *(Moll listens to noise outside)* Go on now. Off ye go.
Bridgie	I'll be looking forward to it, and pray that I'll be guided right.
	(Exit Bridgie)
Moll	Ulick?
	(Ulick pauses)
Moll	Take it nice and easy at the start. If you get over the first fence without a fall you'll finish the course no bother.
Ulick	There's no fear of a fall. I'd say she was often saddled before.
	(Exit Ulick)

End of Act One

56

ACT TWO

Scene 1

Action takes place in the dining cum sitting-room of the presbytery. The Canon is sitting in a comfortable chair near the fire, while Moll arranges table for supper. The Canon smokes his pipe. In the distance can be heard the voices of men and women singing the Adoremus ... .

Moll	I can put up the supper any time Canon.
Canon Pratt	We'll wait Moll, 'til Father Loran is finished with the choir practice. That was a great idea of yours to get a choir going.
Moll	Thank you Canon.
Canon Pratt	Do you like hymns Moll?
Moll	I do Canon, but hymns are sad.
Canon Pratt	That's just the way Father Loran's choir sings them. How long are you here now Moll?
Moll	*(Laying table)* Gone the twelve months Canon.
Canon Pratt	Gone the twelve months. That bingo was a great idea too altogether. The bare year gone by and the church is repaired, the foundations for the school are dug and work will start next week. I never thought I'd live to see the day. The Bishop is your happy man. Did I tell you he complimented me on the fund-raising?

57

Moll   Did he now?

Canon Pratt   He told me I was a credit to the diocese. I'm very mindful, said he, of good builders and I'm very thankful, said he, to priests who build modern schools. I often think of them, he said.

Moll   (*Repeats*) He often think of them. What did he mean by that, I wonder?

Canon Pratt   You never know till after what a Bishop means Moll, as many a poor priest knows to his cost. All we can do is hope for the best. Still and all, the outlook is good and God is good too.

Moll   God knows but 'tis fine for you. 'Tis how you'll wind up Bishop one day yourself.

Canon Pratt   Doubtful Moll, but men were made Monsignors and Archdeacons with far less to their credit.

Moll   'Tis fine for some.

Canon Pratt   (*Looks at her suspiciously*) Am I right in thinking we have a touch of the sulks today ...? Come on Moll. You know me. Out with it, whatever it is.

Moll   I don't know should I Canon.

Canon Pratt   Sit down Moll.

                    (*Moll takes a seat*)

Canon Pratt   Now let's have it. 'Tis always better to get a thing out. And you know me .... It won't pass my lips whatever it is. You may talk to me in complete confidence.

Moll   'Tis money Canon.

Canon Pratt   There are other things in the world besides money girl. There is the grace of God which is more important than all the wealth and all the riches of the five continents put together.

Moll   True for you Canon but couldn't a person have the grace of God and have a bit of money beside it?

Canon Pratt   Spell it out to me Moll.

Moll   I won't put a tooth in it Canon. Security, my own security has me worried sick. I'm getting old Canon and you're not getting any younger yourself so 'tis time I thought about what I would do should anything happen to you. I'd be worse off than a widow.

Canon Pratt   Worse than a widow?

Moll   She would have her widow's pension. I wouldn't have a copper to get from anyone. It's not fair Canon.

Canon Pratt   You shouldn't worry Moll. If anything happens to me you won't be forgotten. You'll get your severance pay. That will be seen to — and fifty pounds of a gift in my will to you.

Moll   Fifty pounds?

Canon Pratt	In black and white.
Moll	By God, you're a gay man with your fifty pounds — 'twould hardly buy a bicycle.
Canon Pratt	What would you say Moll, if I increased it to a hundred?
Moll	You can do the same with that as you did with the fifty — you'll have to do more.
Canon Pratt	Such as?
Moll	Such as a pension scheme and a bulk sum. Everyone gets them these days, and I'm as much entitled to them as the next person.
Canon Pratt	I've never heard the like! A bulk sum and a pension scheme? One would think you were a teacher or a higher civil servant.
Moll	If I were married to you wouldn't I have a life insurance on you? If I was your daughter wouldn't you have to give me a fortune?
Canon Pratt	We'll see, we'll see — a pension now is a different matter.
Moll	Them curates had a right hare made out of you before I came — you were up to your neck in debts and you were run off your feet. 'Twas me that done the worryin' and 'twas me that took charge of the bingo and the raffles. I would be

	expecting a pension of seven or eight pounds a week and a thousand pounds in a bulk sum.
Canon Pratt	A thousand pounds? Tell me 'tis a nightmare I'm having — Where would I get a thousand pounds?
Moll	I'll show you how to make it …. You can take my word for it Canon, that there's a lot more in this parish than you'd think. There's them that lets on to be poor would buy and sell you. What are the people paying into Mass at present?
Canon Pratt	Two new pence.
Moll	*(Dismisses it)* That's nothing short of scandalous. Coppers for Mass, ten shillings for the dance hall. If Monsignor MacMerrigan was here he'd have 'em skinned while you'd be lookin' around you. He was a great warrant to gauge the amount of cash in a parish … and to get it out of 'em.

The Monsignor would never go to a pulpit. *(Imitating him)* 'I don't want to divorce myself from the people', he used to say. 'The minute I go there Moll,' he used to say, 'I leave their world'. The Monsignor knew all the tricks …. He'd saunter out nice and easy, and lean back against the altar, like he'd be after meeting you in the street. Then he'd give the blessing, careless and gay and then he'd stick the two hands into the trouser pockets ….

(Canon follows this and imitates all the actions seriously)

Moll

He had a fine, soft, deep voice; very oily and greasy …. 'Well, well, well, well,' he'd say, 'here we are again. What's this I'm after taking out of my trousers pocket? Ah, it's a penny! I will give this penny to this lovely girl in the front seat — but wait a minute! What an old fool I am! A penny is no use to her. If she wanted to buy sweets or an apple or an ice cream a penny would be worthless. I had better give her a shilling …. So now, in the honour of God, when you come to Mass next Sunday leave the pennies at home and bring a piece of silver with you. I'll be standing at the gate myself so don't blackguard me. I'm too old for it. I don't deserve it. Forget about today. We can all make mistakes. Just get this clear; I don't want to see anyone make a mistake on Sunday next. Remember, no coppers.' *(Turns up to right)*

Canon Pratt

Did it work?

Moll

Did it what! The following Sunday the Mass contributions were trebled, and it was the same every Sunday after that. Go on Canon, give it a go yourself.

(The Canon steps forward and adopts the Monsignor's pose. He begins confidently enough but soon degenerates into a mutter)

Canon Pratt

Well, well, well, well, here we are again.

What's this I have in my trouser pocket?
A penny, what have I in my other pocket? Why it's a shilling, five new pence.
A penny in one hand and a shilling in
the other. Um…. *(He peters out)* We must
go over it a few times.

Moll   Don't worry you'll have it right for
Sunday. And another thing Canon, them
cards are a right money spinner.

Canon Pratt   Good Lord Moll, now you're not sug-
gesting a poker school?

Moll   Not the playing cards — the Mass cards.

Canon Pratt   What about the Mass cards Moll?

Moll   I don't know where to start Canon.

Canon Pratt   Start at the beginning Moll.

Moll   Father Brest signed nine yesterday morning for the McGoory funeral, while you
were saying Mass. That's nine pounds.

Canon Pratt   Nine pounds in a morning. That's migh-
ty money.

Moll   It should be your money Canon.

Canon Pratt   He says the Masses Moll. He's entitled to
the money.

Moll   Twelve times I had to answer the door
for the pair of them. Most people want-
ing to get you to sign.

Canon Pratt   *(Thoughtfully)* That's twelve pounds be-
tween them.

Moll	And when you came back how many did you sign yourself Canon?
Canon Pratt	Well now Moll, I didn't sign twelve anyway or anything near it, I may tell you.
Moll	That's what I thought Canon.
Canon Pratt	(*Cutely*) And what would you recommend Moll?
Moll	'Tisn't for me to say Canon.
Canon Pratt	Maybe not Moll but I may tell you I value your advice. You won't put me astray at any rate.
Moll	I'm only suggesting now, mind you.
Canon Pratt	I'm here for suggestions girl.
Moll	If you were to sign a big bundle of Mass cards and give them to me, I needn't be sending people away, saying you're not in or telling them to call back again. When I tell them you'll be back later they say Father Brest will do or Father Loran will do. That's honest money out of your pocket Canon ... honest money .... You're losing hundreds Canon ... hundreds ....
Canon Pratt	(*Alarmed*) Hundreds! Faith, I suppose I am.
Moll	Hundreds Canon. 'Tis not unnatural for a person to be fond of money Canon ... to want money in the pocket so that the

house can be run and the parish can be run and all of us paid our wages. 'Tis you that pays them Canon and 'tis no wonder you'd need money Canon. 'Tisn't for yourself you want it.

Canon Pratt 'Tis not indeed.

Moll 'Tis no sin Canon.

Canon Pratt 'Tis no sin Moll. So whoever would come to the door with money for a Mass card you would be there to meet them with the signed card.

Moll 'Tis me always answers the door Canon.

Canon Pratt 'Tis a good idea God knows, but isn't there a danger Moll, that you would give my signed cards to those who would be seeking Father Brest or Father Loran?

Moll I suppose it could happen alright Canon. We all makes mistakes.

Canon Pratt God help us but we do Moll. I'm sure you wouldn't do anything deliberate. You're not the sort as we all know well. (*Rubs chin*) The more I think of it the more I like it.

Moll People set more store in a card signed by a Canon than in a card signed by a curate.

Canon Pratt I'll sign the cards first thing in the morning Moll.

Moll	(*Producing a bundle of cards*) Sure sign a few of them now Canon, it will give you an appetite for your supper.
Canon Pratt	… and about our little problem ….
Moll	We'll go to a solicitor and get him to draw up an agreement.
Canon Pratt	I make no promises, mind you, but allowing I could raise the thousand, I still think it's too much …. We'll talk about it tomorrow.
Moll	I won't be here tomorrow morning! I'm shoving on. I'll go out in the world and find an old man that will marry me.
Canon Pratt	Moll!
Moll	An old man to marry me Canon, and the older the better, because if the heart gives out on him I'll have my widow's pension, and that's a damn sight better than I'll ever see from you with your shining shoes and purple, and your grace of God.
Canon Pratt	The Bishop would have to be consulted….
Moll	Will the Bishop carry the breakfast up to bed to you tomorrow morning?
Canon Pratt	I'll see what can be done.
Moll	There's no seeing, you'll do it or you won't do it. If you do it I'll stay and if you don't do it I won't stay.

Canon Pratt	Be reasonable.
Moll	(*Collects duster, half goes*) I'll say goodbye to you before I go and pack my bags. All I can say is I hope you'll be lucky, and that you'll be minded half as well as I minded you.
Canon Pratt	Wait! Wait a minute! Sit down, sit. It's bad to be hasty.
Moll	It is Canon. You look after me, and I'll look after you. Look at the thousands I'll collect for you in Mass card money — sure there isn't a woman in Ireland would do as well by you.
Canon Pratt	Alright, I'll do it, but you'll have to show me how. I haven't a penny, I swear it.
Moll	That's easy done. (*Stands*) Tomorrow we'll go to a solicitor and get him to draw up an agreement that whoever is parish priest after you must pay me the pension — that's important — and we'll go to the bank and raise the thousand. You'll have no bother. A parish priest's word is stronger than the Rock of Gibraltar. There's no bank manager in the world would refuse you. You put the thousand in your own name and mine with the proviso that if anything happens to you I claim it.
Canon Pratt	And if anything happens to you I can claim it.
Moll	Yes. Set yourself down there now and

put your autograph on that bundle and I'll go fetch the supper.

(*Moll goes to leave as the Canon busies himself but on second thoughts she returns*)

Moll Er .... 'Tis a job you wouldn't expect me to do for nothing Canon.

Canon Pratt How's that Moll?

Moll Giving out the cards and collecting the money for you .... There's a lot of responsibility.

Canon Pratt I'm not sure I understand you.

Moll A commission Canon?

Canon Pratt A commission would be totally unprecedented. I declare to God but I never heard the like.

Moll You won't lose by it Canon.

Canon Pratt What sort of commission?

Moll A shilling in the pound, sure 'tis only five new pence. 'Tisn't much.

Canon Pratt Moll, it's totally unprecedented.

Moll I used to get if from Monsignor Mac Merrigan.

Canon Pratt In that case I see no reason why you shouldn't get it from me. Five pence in the pound it will be.

Moll I'll go and get the supper now Canon.

Canon Pratt	Will you give Father Brest a call Moll?
Moll	I will to be sure Canon and would you ever ask those two buckos to tidy out their rooms? They're in an awful state altogether.
Canon Pratt	And Moll?
Moll	Yes Canon.
Canon Pratt	Call him easy. He says your voice is affecting his eardrums.
Moll	I'll call him like he was a baby Canon. He's a pure baba, God help us.

(Moll laughs and is joined by the Canon. Exit Moll calling out at the top of her voice)

Moll	*(Off)* Father Bre-est ... Father Bre-est ... your supper is on the table ....

(Enter Father Loran)

Canon Pratt	And how's the choir going Father?
Father Loran	Did you ever spend two hours in a rookery Canon?
Canon Pratt	Patience Father, patience. We can't all be Carusos. These are simple people with no musical background. 'Tisn't a cathedral we have.
Father Loran	Is it true you'll be getting a new organ for the Church?
Canon Pratt	We'll have to ask Moll about that.

Father Loran	Moll? Does she know something about organs?
Canon Pratt	I wouldn't say so but I'd say she knows something about the price of them.
Father Loran	We'd badly want a new organ.
Canon Pratt	Why don't you talk to her yourself about it?
Father Loran	I did.
Canon Pratt	And what did she say?
Father Loran	She said I could have it if I had the price of it.
Canon Pratt	And have you the price of it?
Father Loran	I haven't the price of a mouth organ.
Canon Pratt	I like it when a man bares his soul and says his piece.
Father Loran	You do?
Canon Pratt	Of course.
Father Loran	You like music don't you?
Canon Pratt	I like a good song and I like the fiddle played softly.
Father Loran	That's not what I mean. What I mean is a massive choir drawn from the people of this parish. We don't have to confine ourselves to church music, you know.
Canon Pratt	You mean good rousing choruses like

	you'd hear in the pubs of a Saturday night.
Father Loran	No. I do not. I mean one hundred men and one hundred women singing the Mass. Think of Schubert, think of Handel, think of the effect ....
Canon Pratt	I don't know about Schubert, but you're off your handle alright. Do you think the people of this parish have nothing better to do?
Father Loran	It could be done.
Canon Pratt	Choirs are alright for women that have their families reared or for young nuns that are in danger of deserting.
Father Loran	We could give it a trial.
Canon Pratt	Sure .... But wait till you have your own parish.
Father Loran	When I have my own parish I'll have the greatest choir ever heard.
Canon Pratt	By the time you have your own parish you won't have the energy.
Father Loran	*(Places hand across stomach)* By the Lord I'm hungry. Is she looking after the supper?
Canon Pratt	We were waiting on you. She's gone calling Father Brest.
Father Loran	Softly, I noticed.

Canon Pratt	Now, now there's no call for sarcasm. I don't know what's gotten into the pair of you this past year.
Father Loran	I'm not prepared to discuss it Canon. I'm too weak. Discussion might only weaken me further. I'll die young. You'll find me in my bed some morning with my tongue hanging out.

(Enter Father Brest. He seems older somehow and not as spruce as he was. His grooming is not what it was. He is bedraggled. When he enters he goes to fireplace where he elaborately extracts two gobs of cotton wool from his ears)

Father Brest	I was upstairs resting from the fatigue of last night's bingo. Faintly, most melodiously in the distance, the gentle voices of Father Loran's choristers sweetly assailed my ears. Ah, said I, this is sweet peace that cannot last. *(Laughs bitterly)* How right I was. Suddenly the awful shriek of Moll Kettle came to rend the silence apart. The birds were hushed. Time says I for my cotton wool.
Father Loran	Does it soften the blow?
Father Brest	Only a little. Nothing my dear Father, is proof against the rasping screech of our dear housekeeper.
Canon Pratt	Ah!

(Enter Moll bearing plates)

Moll	*(Loudly)* Was you asleep Father Brest?

72

Father Brest	Luckily! No.
Moll	And how is the eardrums this evening?
Father Brest	*(Looks towards Canon)* And pray who told you about my eardrums?
Moll	*(Putting down food)* Sure the whole parish knows about them. Come on the supper will be cold.
Father Brest	And what array of delicacies are we to behold this evening?
Canon Pratt	*(Rising, rubbing his hands and taking his seat happily at table)* It's scrambled eggs on toast and it looks good. Come on lads, sit down. Fetch the tea Moll.
Moll	Here boybawn. Have a look at that while your havin' your supper.
Father Brest	What is it?
Moll	'Tis a catalogue for the most up to date bingo ball dispensers. Turn to page fourteen and tell me what you see.

(Brest does so)

Moll	That bingo machine dispenses bingo balls of every hue. Black balls, blue balls, green balls, balls for every colour of the rainbow.

(Exits)

(Both curates seat themselves. The Canon says grace and is answered by the curates. The Canon immediately plunges into

supper. Father Brest produces a pair of glasses, dons them and inspects plate with great care)

Father Brest   What a way for an innocent egg to end up. I'm glad I'm not the hen that laid it. *(Locates slice of bread and commences to butter it. He nibbles)*

(Enter Moll with teapot. She rests it on the table. Father Brest's eyes are glued to his plate)

Moll   *(To Brest)* Did you lose something Father?

Father Brest   Only my appetite.

Moll   Ha! You poor man, without an eardrum or an appetite.

(Exit Moll)

Father Brest   *(Squirming, to Canon)* Did you hear that? Did you hear that Canon?

Canon Pratt   Eat your supper, like a good man.

Father Brest   You call this mess a supper.

Father Loran   Easy Phil, easy.

Canon Pratt   *(Fed up)* What in blazes do you want? Tell us and we'll get it for you. Anything to put an end to this perpetual whining.

Father Brest   All I want is a decent meal. I want nothing fancy.

Canon Pratt   The Lord save us, there are millions

starving in India and South America ...

Father Loran   And Peru ....

Canon Pratt   And Peru. Do you ever think of them?

Father Brest   You think of them. I have enough of a problem trying to stay alive myself.

Canon Pratt   *(Clucks tongue)* Will you like a good man, will you pour out the tea Father Loran?

(Father Loran proceeds to pour tea)

Father Brest   *(Change of tactics)* Look we are three grown men and there's no reason why we should be at loggerheads. Don't you agree Canon?

Canon Pratt   *(Eager to heal friction)* That's what I'm always saying. If we can't iron out our differences at our age we have failed in our calling. By God Phil, I'm with you all the way. Let us try to pull together rather than apart.

Father Loran   Wisely put Canon. As the hymn says — You'll never walk alone.

Canon Pratt   Yes thank you. That's the spirit. Back to the good old days again, eh. Huh? Huh?

Father Brest   I hope so Canon. I fervently hope so. But to reach any degree of happiness in any walk of life certain little sacrifices, certain acts of kindness and thoughtfulness are called for, especially if this little community of ours is to be restored to that happy state we once knew. Right?

Father Loran	Right.
Canon Pratt	Right.
Father Brest	What I want to know *Father*, is who should make the first sacrifice. Who should set the example. *(Indicates Canon)* Would you say it should come from the top or the bottom?
Father Loran	Oh, the top ... the top ... where else?
Father Brest	And who is the top? Who is the leader in this house?
Father Loran	Moll Kettle.
Father Brest	Don't be facetious. Our leader is our Canon.
Father Loran	Of course. *(Shouts towards kitchen)* Sorry Moll.
Father Brest	I have already made my sacrifice. I run a regular bingo session. That, to me, is the greatest sacrifice of all.
Canon Pratt	That's not a sacrifice. That is an elementary parish duty, an evening chore.
Father Brest	You're wrong. For me it is the great sacrifice *(Shouts)* because I hate the damned thing. I detest it. I loathe and despise it. I have frequent nightmares that are filled with numbers ... red twenty-eight, green twenty-two, yellow fourteen, black forty-six ....
Father Loran	No. No. No, black forty-seven.

76

Father Brest	Black forty-seven?
Father Loran	Don't you get it … *(Points at plate)* the hunger … the starvation …? The great famine.
Father Brest	Bingo will eventually be the death of me. I have become resigned to it. You have heard of the Cisco Kid the Sundance Kid, not forgetting Billy the Kid but here before you is the original … one and only … Bingo Kid.
Canon Pratt	Might I ask what you are driving at Father?
Father Brest	Certainly Canon. I am going to ask you, in the interests of harmony, to make a little sacrifice.
Canon Pratt	I'll go a reasonable length to restore harmony. What is it you expect of me?
Father Brest	From now on Canon, I want you to swap plates with me.
	(There is a silence as this sinks in. Canon slowly lowers napkin with which he has been wiping his mouth. Canon's eyes fall to his own plate, slowly and move to Brest's)
Father Brest	It's not much. I shall endeavour to do full justice to your plate and while you are doing full justice to mine you can devote a little thought to the starving millions who are causing so much concern. *(To Loran)* What do you think Father?

77

Father Loran	It seems fair. It's not as if you were asking the Canon to forego his meals. He will have yours.
	(Canon shattered)
Father Brest	Exactly. Nobody can say it's unreasonable. What do you say Canon? Are you prepared to make this small sacrifice?
Canon Pratt	I see nothing small about it.
Father Brest	You don't infer then that my plate is not an adequate swap for yours?
Canon Pratt	I didn't say that.
Father Brest	Then you agree.
Canon Pratt	Of course I agree. I've always set the lead in this presbytery.
Father Loran	Hear. Hear. *(Hand on his shoulder)* Canon, you have taken the first important step towards a lasting peace. Would that the great powers of the world had half your courage at their peace talks.
Canon Pratt	I do what I can.
Father Loran	*(Carried away)* Let's shake hands on it.
	(All shake)
Canon Pratt	*(Standing, rubs hands)* Ah, this is great. I am very happy lads, very happy indeed. And now I'm going to ask the two of you to make a little sacrifice ….
Father Loran	Anything Canon, anything.

Canon Pratt	As you both know Moll is not getting younger. What she really needs is a little serving girl to do the beds and shine the windows.
Father Brest	Yes of course.
Canon Pratt	She refuses, however, to allow a girl inside the door. The poor woman is genuinely overworked and God knows 'tis hardly fair to her if you know what I mean ….
Father Brest	What do you mean Canon?
Canon Pratt	Suppose the two of you were to make your own beds and be responsible for the tidiness of your own rooms. She says that this would be a great help to her.
Father Brest	Canon I am a priest not a parlour maid … I … I ….
Father Loran	Take it easy Phil. It's not so awful. Any fool can make a bed. It's reasonable enough.
Canon Pratt	Well Philip?
Father Brest	Alright. I won't spoil sport.
Canon Pratt	(Sits) There are good times coming. Thanks be to the good God, say I.
	(Enter Moll)
Moll	There's some apple pie and custard if anyone would care for some.

79

Father Brest   Bring it on woman. Bring it on. *(Rubbing hands and going to table)*

(Exit Moll)

Father Brest   *(Sitting down, spoon in one hand, fork in the other)* Even as a child I had a particular longing for apple pie and custard. My mother used to specialise in apple pies. I must get her to send you one Canon.

Canon Pratt   That would be nice.

Father Brest   *(Extremely good cheer)* We had our own orchard, still have in fact. It's a wonder you never thought of planting a few fruit trees Canon.

Canon Pratt   No time.

Father Brest   There's a good market for fresh fruit.

(Enter Moll, bearing a tray on which there are three dessert plates. She places one in front of each, the Canon first, Father Loran second, and Father Brest third)

Moll   *(To Canon)* One for the master. *(Places plate in front of him)* One for the Dame. *(She places plate in front of him)* And one for the little boy that lives down the lane. *(She places largest plate in front of Father Brest)*

Father Brest   *(Rubs his hands)* This is fabulous. This is the loveliest and the largest dish of apple pie and custard I have ever seen. Thank you Moll.

Moll   Don't mention it Father.

Father Brest   *(Seizing spoon and adjusting himself on chair)* This is really something.

(The Canon coughs politely in Father Brest's direction)

Father Brest   Yes Canon?

(The Canon points at Father Brest's plate and then points at himself with a most polite smile. Father Brest is puzzled. Canon hands his plate to Father Brest. Brest accepts it, still wondering. Then it dawns on him. He lifts his own plate and reluctantly hands it to the Canon who accepts it cheerily. Canon wires into it watched by Brest and Loran. Moll laughs and exits)

Bridge ACT TWO Scene 1 to Scene 2

Canon Pratt

They happen all around us every day but mostly we don't even recognise them. I am talking about God's little miracles. *(Enter Bridgie, heavily pregnant)* There's a saying to cover it, what in blazes is it now...? Oh, yes, 'God works in mysterious ways'. You've often heard that said, no doubt. Well, 'tis none the less true for that.

Sure who'd have thought that Father Loran, a man without the echo of a note in his head, would be after running a choir? God alone knows. And He must have given the hint to Moll Kettle for wasn't it she who organised it?

Oh, yes, there was a great deal of honest activity going on in Ballast during Moll's time at the presbytery. And thanks be to God, says I.

Moll reads the paper by the fire. Father Brest tries fixing his bingo machine.

Moll

(Referring to the paper) There's a picture in here of the new school. Wasn't it a lucky day the Canon hired me four years ago! Look what I done. I built as fine a school as you'd see in Ireland and today 'tis being opened. 'Tis a great pity the Bishop can't be here ... but sure we can't have everything.

Father Brest	You really think it was you and you alone who built the school?
Moll	'Twas me and the bingo.
Father Brest	Bingo … the ultimate role of the Catholic Church in Ireland … the propagation of bingo.
Moll	May God forgive you.
Father Brest	Where's the Canon?
Moll	Bed.
Father Brest	This hour of the day? Is he sick or what?
Moll	He's fine boybawn, thanks be to God. He's resting for the celebrations. I don't see your name here.
Father Brest	Where?
Moll	The new list of diocesan appointments.
Father Brest	How in the name of God would my name be there when old fogies of eighty and more won't give up the ghost? You'd think they would have the grace to retire and give the younger men a chance.
Moll	A chance at what?
Father Brest	A chance to prove ourselves, to bring decaying parishes up-to-date, to get with it.
Moll	A lot you did with this decaying parish until I arrived and a lot you'd do now if you were let at it yourself. Where would you get the money?

Father Brest	*(Bluffing)* God is good.
Moll	And bingo is good and raffles is good and jumble sales is good.
Father Brest	*(Getting up)* Yirra, jumble rubbish …. By the way, did you see my golf clubs anywhere?
Moll	Golf clubs? Yirra you have no time for golf boybawn, the man that has 'em now has his handicap down to nine.
Father Brest	Haw?
Moll	And they raised three ten for the new school.
Father Brest	Do you mean to stand there and tell me …?
Moll	Yirra blast you, what do I care about you?
Father Brest	That's a nice way to address a priest.
Moll	If you don't learn how to master that contraption your balls will be all over the place tonight.
Father Brest	Oh dear God but you're a terrible creature altogether but the Church will master you in the end.
Moll	And pray what have I to do with the Church? Sure an altar boy is higher up in the Church than I am.
Father Brest	There's one great consolation.

Moll What would that be?

Father Brest When the Canon's day comes you're for the high jump. You'll go the road of Hitler and Stalin and all the other tyrants.

Moll If I do I'll have something to show for my time.

Father Brest You don't have to tell me. By God you must have a right few quid made out of the Mass cards *(Looking back at her)* not to mention the butcher and the baker and the grocer and any place else you could rob a halfpenny.

Moll *(Strong)* I have as much rights as you have and when *(Sly)* you're going to the Bishop let me know and I'll go with you. And if you're not satisfied with the Bishop we'll go to the Cardinal and if you're not satisfied with the Cardinal we'll go to the Pope.

Father Brest You're mad, stone mad.

Moll Come on. You're the one that wanted to go to the Bishop, aren't you? Always talking about it behind my back. Come on and we'll tell him that there's a new school since I came to this parish and we'll tell him the church is repaired and all the debts paid, all since I came.

Father Brest It was our work, mine and Father Loran's.

(Enter Father Loran, coatless and wearing

dust turban. He carries a vacuum cleaner under his arm and a mop and pail in his hand)

Father Loran   I've just done my room. Do you want me to do yours?

Father Brest   No thank you.

Father Loran   I'll give it a hoover so.

Father Brest   I'm alright. I told you I can pull my weight.

Father Loran   You mustn't fret yourself.

Father Brest   I'm not fretting myself. *(Indicates Moll)* This monster here has me upset. She won't rest happy 'til she has me under the clay.

Father Loran   Now, now, Phil, you mustn't let her get at you. I just ignore her.

Moll   Listen to the Mohammedan with the turban on his poll. A pity the Bishop couldn't see you now.

Father Loran   *(Mustering dignity)* Varium et mutabile semper femina.

Father Brest   Well spoken Father Loran.

Moll   *(In spite)* In nomina domina gomina, goose-grease galorum, sago lumbago tapioca semolina and if you don't like the music you can change the band, and if you're going to do any hoovering here boybawn forget it. I want to have a snooze before the festivities.

(Father Loran hoovers; Father Brest busies himself about his bingo machine and Moll after a few moments looking at the paper appears to doze off. As the hoovering stops Brest and Loran are struck by the silence in the room and eventually focusing on Moll they realise she is asleep, the newspaper covering her face)

Father Brest   Look at her. You'd swear butter wouldn't melt in her mouth. The devil incarnate.

Father Loran   The devil?

Father Brest   Who but a devil or an evil spirit would interfere with my sermon on mixed marriages? 'Mixed marriages how are you' says she "twould be more in your line to give a sermon on mixed bread'.

Father Loran   *(Now moving in closer to Moll)* Phil, maybe she is possessed.

Father Brest   The devil has more sense.

Father Loran   No seriously, she's dozing. This may be the only chance we ever have to exorcise her.

(Father Brest is about to protest but Loran is gone like a shot to get the accoutrements for the exorcism. Brest remains sceptical but interested throughout the following. Loran re-enters wearing purple stole and carrying a lit candle and holy water font and sprinkler. Still wearing the apron and

turban from his cleaning duties, he cuts a bizarre figure)

Father Brest
I don't like this one bit. Maybe it might be better if we made contact with the official diocesan exorcist.

Father Loran
He'd never agree and she'd never submit. We'd have to tie her down.

Father Brest
Suppose something goes wrong!

Father Loran
It's a chance we have to take. Look it's for her own good. There's no doubt but she's possessed. There's no other explanation for her diabolical behaviour. Here ... hold this.

(He hands him holy water vat and sprinkler. Father Loran finds book in his vestments and, wetting his thumb, locates appropriate page. He approaches Moll and removes the newspaper. She stirs uneasily but does not wake. Solemnly Father Loran dips his sprinkler into the holy water vat. Moll opens her eyes while their backs are turned, looks up and falls quickly back to pretended sleep again)

Father Brest
The room first.

(Father Loran dutifully sprinkles the entire room before addressing himself to Moll. He mutters some Latin while sprinkling. He gently sprinkles Moll. She stirs but does not waken)

Father Brest
Easy for God's sake.

Father Loran   O Lord we call on you now in our hour of great need, to rescue us from Satan and his minions. We ask you to free your poor servant Moll Kettle from the devil's tricks, that she might return to the path of goodness, gentleness, meekness.

(Moll opens her eyes and staring demoniacally at Brest and Loran chases them from the room. Collapses laughing in the chair as the Canon enters)

Canon Pratt   I brought you these empties, save you the trouble of getting them yourself.

Moll   There was no need to do that. Sit down by the fire and read your paper.

Canon Pratt   Anything good in it?

Moll   The Pope says the world has gone to the dogs.

Canon Pratt   My mother used to say the same thing when I was a child.

Moll   People has no conscience these days.

Canon Pratt   Too well I know it.

Moll   Where's it going to end Canon, with the women going around half naked?

(Canon clucks tongue reproachfully and nods his head in agreement)

Moll   They'll be wearing nothing at all soon.

Canon Pratt   The country is too cold for that.

Moll   When I was a girl, walking the streets with my friends, you would hear the hum of the holy Rosary from every home.

Canon Pratt   My God, yes.

Moll   And the beads rattling like horses' tackling. 'Tis the Beatles you'd hear now.

(The Canon settles himself in his chair and reads his newspaper. There's a momentary lull)

Canon Pratt   Where were Fathers Brest and Loran rushing off to Moll?

Moll   *(Twinkle in her eye)* The divil only knows Canon.

Canon Pratt   They're very agitated these days Moll.

Moll   The Lord save us all Canon, there's no meaning in the curates that's going these days. There's none of 'em want to do what they're told. Father Brest is as bold as brass. God be with the fine curates we had when I was young. Pure saints they were with the eyes gone back in their heads and black rings under them like they'd be painted. Skin and bone and thin white faces, with the cheekbones standing out like corpses. 'Tis they were the holy men and 'twasn't their bellies was troubling them.

Canon Pratt   'Twas not indeed.

Moll	I remember one of Monsignor Mac Merrigan's first curates. You would swear he was after being whitewashed, the creature was so pale. He couldn't talk, only whisper. The Lord save us, but I tried every shop in the diocese to find a collar small enough for his neck. Sure he had no neck Canon. 'Twas all Adam's apple. I often saw him stagger with the weakness of a winter's morning ....
Canon Pratt	Where's he now Moll?
Moll	He's in heaven Canon. Where the hell else would he be!
Canon Pratt	Where else indeed, the poor man.
Moll	A Canon now is different.
Canon Pratt	What should he be like now Moll? *(Preens himself)*
Moll	He should be fat and pleasant with a fine red face and a deep voice, like a bull, to frighten the sinners and to give the people confidence. Sure you would never see a thin Canon. What would the people think if he wasn't round and shining and in prime condition.
Canon Pratt	Go on, go on.
Moll	A Canon now should be a fine, rumbling, thundering man, well-fed and groomed so that his parish could boast of his appearance and be proud of him. He should have a fine thick neck, a

severe face and a noble bearing to give him weight and holiness. Yourself now Canon, is a fine example of what a Canon should look like. Show me the priest, the Monsignor used to say, and I'll tell you what the parish is like.

Canon Pratt   (*Preens himself*) I dare say there's a lot in what you say Moll. God knows you're not a woman that's given to exaggeration. I suppose there's no one would say that I'm not cut out for my job.

Moll   There's no one would deny it Canon, no one. God save us but them curates of ours are a pure disgrace, that would eat you out of house and home instead of fasting and abstaining like the saints and martyrs.

Canon Pratt   Now, now, Moll, we mustn't be hard.

Moll   When I was handing up Brest his dinner the day you were away, he says to me, 'Where's the soup?' 'What soup is that boybawn?' I said to him. 'The soup before lunch', says he. 'Soup is for invalids', I told him. 'That's me', says he. I tell you Canon, when they start looking for soup before their dinner, they'll be looking for it after their dinner, sure isn't soup a dinner in itself Canon?

Canon Pratt   A good plate of soup can be most nourishing.

(*Enter Father Brest in an excited state*)

Father Brest	The Bishop! The Bishop!
Canon Pratt	What about the Bishop?
Father Brest	The Bishop, he's coming.
Canon Pratt	Sure he can't be coming, sure isn't he way out foreign someplace.
Father Brest	Well he's here now.
Canon Pratt	Oh Moll, there's nothing ready.
Moll	Calm down Canon, calm down.
Father Loran	His Lordship the Bishop.

(Enter a Bishop in full regalia and humour. He is the master of the diocese)

Bishop *(To Moll and Canon)* Don't stand up. Don't stand up. You're looking well Connie. *(Expansively. As the Canon kisses his ring)* None of that. No need for that.

Canon Pratt A drink Moll. Get a drink for his Lordship. A drink for everybody. Paddy Flaherty isn't it my Lord?

Bishop Yes. A drop of Paddy. Take a little wine Saint Paul says, for thy stomach's sake and for thy frequent infirmities.

(Exit Moll)

Bishop I was in Morocco. I woke up yesterday evening after lunch and looked out over the Mediterranean. This is very nice, very nice, I told myself, but isn't something happening in another part of the world? Isn't a school about to be opened, I said to myself. Isn't it about to be opened in my own diocese and isn't it to be opened by a substitute? Time I said to myself to be hitting for the green isle of Erin. Here I am ....

(All applaud)

Father Loran   Marvellous! Marvellous!

Father Brest   To cut short his holiday.

Canon Pratt   It's what we expect of the man.

Father Loran   Imagine from Morocco to Ballast!

Bishop   *(To Canon)* It's a great credit to you Canon Pratt. Four years ago we had a ramshackle outhouse where you would be ashamed to send a decent scholar. *(To window. Looks out)* Now we have a school second to none. I am not unmindful of builders, those who further the cause of education are always in my mind, if you know what I mean.

(Enter Moll, bearing a tray on which are glasses. Puts tray and glasses on right of table near Bishop. Whiskey on tray. Brest pours out drinks, gives one to Bishop. Moll takes glass off table and gives it to Canon)

Moll   *(Distributing drinks)* Now would anyone like a drop of soup to keep them going 'til the festivities begin?

94

MOLL

Bishop	Pray who have we here?
Canon Pratt	This is our housekeeper my Lord.

(Brest brings Loran down to left and is obviously arguing with him. 'Now is the time', Loran demurs)

Bishop	So this is Moll. *(Puts out hand, Moll kisses ring)*
Canon Pratt	You know of her?
Bishop	*(Retaining Moll's hand)* We know more than we are supposed to know Canon Pratt. *(Slaps her hand)* I have heard great accounts of Moll. *(Pats her shoulder, ushering her off)* Moll, fetch a drink for yourself and then we will all toast the great centre of education which is about to be declared open.
Moll	Yes, my Lord.

(Exit Moll)

Bishop	*(To curates)* And now gentlemen, what's the score with the pair of you?

(Suddenly faces them. Brest rather quickly and suddenly turns)

Father Brest	We're fine, fine, my Lord.
Bishop	No grievances?
Father Loran	No … no … not at all.
Bishop	A presbytery without grievances is paradise. Paradise does not come until we

95

visit the next world. Speak up gentlemen.

Father Loran   *(Prompted by Father Brest)* Well, there's
never a rose without a thorn your Lord-
ship.

Canon Pratt   *(Interjects)* They're always hopping balls
my Lord! Look at them. Did you ever see
such health?

Father Brest   Go on Joe.

*(Loran hesitates. Brest fumes and is about
to explode)*

Father Brest   As the senior curate in this parish I ....

Moll   *(Entering)* Here I am Canon.

Canon Pratt   Will you be toastmaster my Lord? Joe,
will you like a good man get the parish
camera, we'll record this for posterity.
You don't mind my Lord?

Bishop   Certainly not. Moll! *(Bishop beckons Moll
over for photo)*

Moll   Me!

Bishop   Ladies and Gentlemen, I bid you toast
our new school. Long may it stand and
may the scholars pour forth from its
portals until Gabriel sounds his horn.
Go maire sé go deo is go dtiocfaidh na
scoláirí ó na hallaí ina sluaite.

(All quaff. Exit Moll)

Father Brest	My Lord you asked earlier if we had any grievances. Well on our behalf Father Loran would like to say a few words about conditions in this presbytery. Father Loran?
	(Again Loran hesitates)
Bishop	*(To Loran)* Well what have you to say?
Father Loran	What do you want me to say my Lord?
Bishop	Say what's in your mind. Be frank. Be candid.
Father Loran	Be candid about what my Lord?
Bishop	About conditions in this presbytery.
Father Loran	*(Unctuous)* I have no complaints my Lord. I am only a curate.
Father Brest	Only a curate …. Tell him the truth ….
Father Loran	*(All innocence)* The truth is my Lord, that I personally have no complaints to make.
Father Brest	Judas. Judas Iscariot.
Bishop	In a few moments I will be opening a new school, and after that I must go to suppress a Women's Lib movement in Lyracrompane. But I cannot leave unless there is peace in this house.
	In Morocco I had time to think. *(To Canon, turns to Canon)* Canon Pratt you have served this diocese well. You have lived in obscurity in this out-of-the-way place for far too long. You have brought

this parish out of the doldrums. You
have given it a new school, a new status.
You are the kind of Canon who deserves
better. *(Moves to Canon, hand on shoul-
der)* For this reason I am appointing you
to the parish of Saint Andrew in the city.
You'll be happy there. I am sure that in
no time at all you will be made a Monsignor. It will be nice to have you near
me in the city. *(Moves casually back to
table)* Your age and experience will be
assets to the diocese.

*(Enter Moll. Bearing Canon's comb, collar,
surplice, and hat)*

Canon Pratt I don't know what to say ... a Monsignor
... Saint Andrew's .... Am I hearing
things? Moll, do you hear this? We are
bound for the city ....

Bishop *(Turns: definitely)* You didn't hear me
right Father. You are bound for the city.
Moll is not bound anywhere.

Canon Pratt But ....

Bishop *(Hand raised)* Let there be no buts. The
parish of Saint Andrew is run by an
order of nuns.

Canon Pratt But we've been together for so long.

Bishop *(Facing Canon)* The Church is a hard
master Canon, but hard as it is it isn't
half as hard as a community of nuns. I
would face the fires of hell on top of a

bucking bronco before I would face a rampaging reverend mother. Moll stays here. Her assistance will be vital. The new parish priest will have a tough task before him.

Canon Pratt   Have you somebody in mind?

Bishop   Indeed I have. (*Turns: he looks at Father Brest*) You may say I have.

(*Father Brest opens his mouth in astonishment and foolishly points a finger towards himself*)

Father Brest   (*Disbelief*) Me?

Bishop   Who else Father?

(*Father Brest staggers with the shock of it. He is supported by Father Loran*)

Bishop   Father Loran you will now be the senior curate. I will appoint a junior curate in due course.

Father Loran   Is there any hope of a transfer my Lord?

(*Bishop laughs*)

Father Loran   Oh God! If I knew the day I was ordained what was before me I'd have jacked the whole thing up and become a Christian Brother. Anything is better than being a curate.

Father Brest   There are worse things in life Father.

Father Loran   (*Faces Father Brest*) Name them.

Father Brest	We'll have good times now Joe. Not to worry.
Bishop	Well Canon. Shall we be on our way? There's a school to be opened and I'd like to see it first.

(Father Loran opens door. They pass down stage of Father Brest who moves up, if necessary, to make room for them. Bishop goes to door. Canon follows fairly slowly. Father Brest a little to right, where Canon blesses him)

Canon Pratt	Of course my Lord. *(They are about to exit)* Oh, and, Moll — see the new parish priest about that 'little arrangement'.

(Exit Canon)

Father Brest	What 'little arrangement'?
Moll	I'll talk to you later Father.
Bishop	I'm sure you will. Has anyone any more to say? Come on. Now's the time. 'Tis no good talking about a Bishop behind his back. Alright then. May God's blessing be always on your ministry here Father Brest. Be patient with your curates, thankful to your housekeeper and remember that incredible though it may seem now, I was once a curate too. God bless ye.

(Exit Bishop)

Father Loran	You came out of it nicely.

Father Brest	I was the senior curate.
Father Loran	And I the junior.
Father Brest	So long as you remember that we'll get on fine.
Father Loran	I never thought I'd see the day.
Moll	'Twill be the best part of an hour before the school is opened. Will you take a drop of soup? I have it ready.
Father Brest	Alright alright. Let's have some soup

(Exit Moll)

Father Brest	This will be a model parish. The new community centre will be an example to the rest of the country.
Father Loran	Where will you get the money?
Father Brest	I'll get it from the greatest source of all — from bingo. From now on we'll have bingo every night but it will be a bigger and a better bingo.

(Enter Moll with tray and two bowls of soup. One small, one large)

Father Brest	You hear me Moll, a bigger and better bingo.
Moll	I declare to God but you'll make a great parish priest entirely.
Father Loran	How come we have different amounts?

101

Moll	What are you talking about?
Father Loran	He has twice as much soup as I have.
Moll	If you don't like it, leave it.
Father Loran	You saw the amount I got.
Father Brest	In the name of God man I can't be bothered with these trifles. I have a big parish to run. You want to watch yourself, fall into line fast. I have only so much patience. Up to your organ loft and get the hang of this yoke between hymns. Bingo is now part of your job. Off you go now.
Father Loran	A curate's lot is a hard one ... *(Opens door)* there's no doubt but the curates of this country should be canonised. Canonised. *(Exits As bingo balls erupt from the machine)*
Father Brest	It's not going to be easy Moll. That new community centre will cost money.
Moll	Put your legs up there and rest yourself. We have our bingo and what's to stop us having silver circles and raffles? If the money is there we'll get it out of them. You look out for me Father and I'll look out for you and let the curates of this world look after themselves.

Curtain

MORE MERCIER BESTSELLERS

THE FIELD

John B. Keane

THE FIELD is John B. Keane's fierce and tender study of the love a man can have for land and the ruthless lengths he will go to in order to obtain the object of his desire. *Now a major film.*

THE YEAR OF THE HIKER

John B. Keane

The Hiker is the much hated father who deserted his wife and family and whose return is awaited with fear.

THE MAN FROM CLARE

John B. Keane

The personal tragedy of an aging athlete who finds he no longer has the physical strength to maintain his position as captain of the team or his reputation as the best footballer in Clare.

THE BUDS OF BALLYBUNION

John B. Keane

The Buds come to the seaside at Ballybunion for their yearly break. (Bud is the abbreviation of the Irish word, *bodaire* , meaning a rough country person.)

THE CHASTITUTE

John B. Keane

'A Chastitute is a person without holy orders who has never lain down with a woman.' This is the definition given by John B. Keane, who in this amusing play holds up some 'sacred cows' to ridicule.

THE CHANGE IN MAME FADDEN

John B. Keane

A powerful drama depicting a woman facing the change of life, and how her family fail to understand the turmoil she is experiencing.